This Little Tiger book belongs to:

_____

_____

_____

For Oscar and Tavo, the original Buckaroos,
with special thanks to RGG ~ ST

For Rachel, my little sister ~ T K

LITTLE TIGER PRESS
1 The Coda Centre, 189 Munster Road,
London SW6 6AW
www.littletiger.co.uk

First published in Great Britain 2016
This edition published 2016
Text copyright © Shanda Trent 2016
Illustrations copyright © Tom Knight 2016
Shanda Trent and Tom Knight have asserted their rights
to be identified as the author and illustrator of this work
under the Copyright, Designs and Patents Act, 1988
A CIP catalogue record for this book is available
from the British Library

ISBN 978-1-84869-231-2
Printed in China
LTP/1400/1256/0116
2 4 6 8 10 9 7 5 3 1

GiDDY-UP BUCKaROOS!

Shanda Trent

Tom Knight

LITTLE TIGER PRESS
London

Giddy-up, **Buckaroos!**
Here comes the sun.

Let's sneak past the sheriff
and round up some fun.

Grab something tasty,
uno, dos, tres.

No time to clean up.
Gotta scram from this place.

Dash past
the **lobo**

that lives
in his den.

¡Ándale!
Hurry!
We fooled him again!

A stagecoach! Surround it.
Let's holler and hoot.

Now head for the hills
with this sack
full of loot.

Race 'round these barrels
in cloverleaf loops.

Try not to tip them.
¡Qué lástima!
Oops.

The sheriff! She'll catch us.

Whew.
That was close.

¡Qué bueno!
We lost her.

Giddy-up!
¡Adiós!

Out in the desert.
No **agua** in sight.
Is there nothing
to quench us?

Here's something
that might!

Plip-plop goes the rain.

Squish-squoosh goes the mud.

The río is rising.
Oh no! A flash flood!

Rescue that lizard.
We flooded his nest.

Buckaroo heroes,
the best in the West!

Shucks!
It's the sheriff.
No, don't wash
my shirt!

Cowboys take days to
collect all this dirt.

Our bellies are grumbling
for something to eat.

Follow your nose
to a buckaroo treat.

Roast armadillo.

Yum!
Rattlesnake stew.

BREEZY
BEANS

Here, give our amigo a bite of it too.

Listen! What's that?
The sheriff is near!

She'll sneak up
and brand us.

¡Venga!
Hide here.

Uh-oh! We're captured.
We can't get away.

Is this adiós to our buckaroo day?

Off to the bunkhouse,
    we make our retreat.

Hats off our heads,
    and boots off our feet.

The night sky is glowing
with twinkly stars.

We sing with coyotes
and strum our guitars.

We're wrapped in our bedrolls
and snuggled in tight.
Buckaroo bedtime.

Buenas noches,
goodnight.

Glossary

Adiós *(ah-dee-**oss**)* – Goodbye

Agua *(**ah**-gwah)* – Water

Amigo *(ah-**mee**-go)* – Friend

¡Ándale! *(**an**-da-ley)* – Hurry!

Buenas noches

*(**bweh**-nahs **noh**-chehs)* – Goodnight

¡Caramba! *(kah-**rahm**-bah)* – Yikes!

Lobo *(lo-bo)* – Wolf

¡Qué bueno! *(keh **bweh**-no)*

– Excellent!

¡Qué lástima! *(keh **las**-teema)*

– What a shame!

Río *(**ree**-o)* – River

Uno, dos, tres

*(**ooh**-no, **doss**, **trayce**)*– One, two, three

¡Venga! *(**ben**-ga)* – Come on!

Yee-haw! More awesome adventures from Little Tiger Press!

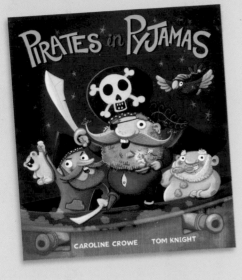

PIRATES in PYJAMAS
CAROLINE CROWE · TOM KNIGHT

The Great Cheese Robbery
Tim Warnes

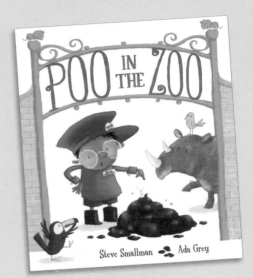

POO IN THE ZOO
Steve Smallman · Ada Grey

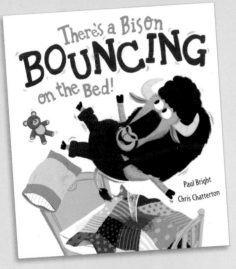

There's a Bison BOUNCING on the Bed!
Paul Bright
Chris Chatterton

A monster's MOVED IN!
TIMOTHY KNAPMAN
LORETTA SCHAUER

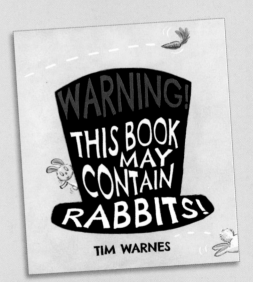

WARNING! THIS BOOK MAY CONTAIN RABBITS!
TIM WARNES

For information regarding any of the above titles
or for our catalogue, please contact us:
Little Tiger Press, 1 The Coda Centre,
189 Munster Road, London SW6 6AW
Tel: 020 7385 6333
E-mail: contact@littletiger.co.uk

www.littletiger.co.uk

Yahoo! Two little cowboys are running riot.

¡Caramba! **watch out!** Don't get caught by the sheriff!

With a sprinkling of Spanish vocabulary!

ISBN 978-1-84869-231-2

9 781848 692312

£6.99

www.littletiger.co.uk

Little Tiger Press